Better Not Get Wet, Jesse Bear

Better Not Get Wet, Jesse Bear

by Nancy White Carlstrom

illustrations by Bruce Degen

Macmillan Publishing Company
New York

Collier Macmillan Publishers
London

By the same author

Jesse Bear, What Will You Wear?
The Moon Came Too
Wild Wild Sunflower Child Anna

Macmillan Publishing Company
866 Third Avenue, New York, NY 10022
Collier Macmillan Canada, Inc.
Printed in the United States of America
First Edition

10 9 8 7 6 5 4 3 2

The text of this book is set in 18 point Goudy Old Style.
The illustrations are rendered in pen-and-ink
and watercolor on paper and reproduced in full color.
Library of Congress Cataloging-in-Publication Data
Carlstrom, Nancy White.
Better not get wet, Jesse Bear.
Summary: Jesse Bear watches all sorts of animals
getting wet on his way to a wading pool where it's
finally all right for him to get wet too.
[1. Bears—Fiction. 2. Stories in rhyme]
I. Degen, Bruce, ill. II. Title.
PZ8.3.C1948Be 1988 [E] 87-10810
ISBN 0-02-717280-5

For Dad
with love
—N.W.C.

For Ben and Sandy,
who love to get wet
—B.D.

Blue cup, blue cup
Drinking all the juice up.

Poking, soaking, hey hey
Getting wet is okay
For you, cup.

Goldfish, goldfish
Swimming with a fin swish.

Flapping, slapping, hey hey
Getting wet is okay
For you, fish.

Red rose, red rose
Sipping from a long hose.

Let me help you take a shower
I can make a sprinkle tower.

Better not get wet, Jesse Bear.

Sipping, dripping, hey hey
Getting wet is okay
For you, rose.

Blackbird, blackbird
Talking with a chirp word.

Let me help you bathe your feathers
We can splatter drops together.

Better not get wet, Jesse Bear.

Splatter, spatter, hey hey
Getting wet is okay
For you, bird.

Brown worm, brown worm
Moving with a warm squirm.

Let me help you crawl along
I can play a puddle song.

Better not get wet, Jesse Bear.

Squirming, turning, hey hey
Getting wet is okay
For you, worm.

Green frog, green frog
Sitting by an old log.

Let me help you with a hop
I can jump and squish and plop.

Better not get wet, Jesse Bear.

Hopping, plopping, hey hey
Getting wet is okay
For you, frog.

White swan, white swan
Gliding on the smooth pond.

Plunking, dunking, hey hey
Getting wet is okay
For you, swan.

Jesse Bear, Jesse Bear
Running, jumping through the air.

Let us help you keep so cool
You can splash in your own pool.

Boating, floating, hey hey
Getting wet is okay
Hooray! Hooray!